MAIN LINE ENGINES

BY THE REV. W. AWDRY

On the Fat Controller's Railway trucks disappear, some bees escape, and a green hat is mistaken for the Guard's flag! Two new mischievous twin engines, Bill and Ben, are introduced to the system and BoCo the diesel is a newcomer too, but how useful he proves to be.

ISBN 0 7182 0420 4

40p NET. (IN UK ONLY)

PRINTED IN ENGLAND

Titles in the series:

1. The Three Railway Engines
2. Thomas the Tank Engine
3. James the Red Engine
4. Tank Engine Thomas Again
5. Troublesome Engines
6. Henry the Green Engine
7. Toby the Tram Engine
8. Gordon the Big Engine
9. Edward the Blue Engine
10. Four Little Engines
11. Percy the Small Engine
12. The Eight Famous Engines
13. Duck and the Diesel Engine
14. The Little Old Engine
15. The Twin Engines
16. Branch Line Engines
17. Gallant Old Engine
18. Stepney the "Bluebell" Engine
19. Mountain Engines
20. Very Old Engines
21. Main Line Engines
22. Small Railway Engines
23. Enterprising Engines
24. Oliver the Western Engine
25. Duke the Lost Engine
26. Tramway Engines

COAL & COKE
1

Railway Series, No. 21

MAIN LINE ENGINES

by

THE REV. W. AWDRY

with illustrations by

PETER AND GUNVOR EDWARDS

KAYE & WARD LIMITED

21 NEW STREET, LONDON EC2M 4NT

First published by Edmund Ward Ltd
1966

Fourth impression by Kaye & Ward Ltd
21 New Street, London EC2M 4NT
1979

ISBN 0 7182 0020 9 (Hardback)
ISBN 0 7182 0420 4 (Paperback)

Printed and bound in Great Britain at William Clowes & Sons Limited
Beccles and London

DEAR FRIENDS,

Bill and Ben are a shameless pair. I meant to write about Main Line Engines, and give the twins a treat by letting them into the first story. But I couldn't keep them in order! Before I knew it they had crept into the others. They even wanted me to change the book and make it about them!

But I have been very firm. I am *still* calling it Main Line Engines. That will serve Bill and Ben right for ragging poor Gordon so disgracefully.

He hasn't got over it yet!

THE AUTHOR

The Diseasel

BILL AND BEN are tank-engines who live at a port on Edward's line. Each has four wheels, a tiny chimney and dome, and a small squat cab.

They are kept busy pulling trucks for ships in the harbour and engines on the main line.

The trucks are filled with China Clay dug from the nearby hills. China Clay is important. It is needed for pottery, paper, paint, plastics, and many other things.

One morning they arranged some trucks and went away for more. They returned to find them all gone.

They were most surprised.

SODOR CHINA CLAYS LTD
BRENDAM
P

Their Drivers examined a patch of oil. "That's a diesel," they said, wiping the rails clean.

"It's a what'll?" asked Bill.

"A diseasel, I think," replied Ben. "There's a notice about them in our Shed."

"I remember, 'Coughs and sneezles spread diseasels.' "

"Who had a cough in his smokebox yesterday?"

"Fireman cleaned it, didn't he?"

"Yes, but the dust made him sneezle: so there you are. It's *your* fault the diseasel came."

"It isn't!"

"It is!"

"Stop arguing, you two," laughed their Drivers. "Come on! Let's go and rescue our trucks."

S C C
BEN
2
S C C

Bill and Ben were aghast. "But he'll magic us away like the trucks."

Their Drivers laughed. "He won't magic us; we'll more likely magic him! Listen. He doesn't know you're twins; so we'll take your names and numbers off and then this is what we'll do . . . "

Bill and Ben chuckled with delight. "Come on! Let's go!" they said eagerly.

Creeping into Edward's Yard they found the diesel on a siding with the missing trucks. Ben hid behind, but Bill went boldly alongside and stood facing the diesel on the points leading out to the main line.

BEN

The diesel looked up. "Do you mind?" he asked.

"Yes," said Bill, "I do. I want my trucks please."

"These are mine," said the diesel. "Go away."

Bill pretended to be frightened. "You're a big bully," he whimpered. "You'll be sorry."

He moved over the points, ran back, and hid behind the trucks on the other side.

Ben now came forward. The diesel had to stop suddenly.

"Truck stealer," hissed Ben. He ran away too, and Bill took his place.

This went on and on till the diesel's eyes nearly popped out.

"Stop!" he begged. "You're making me giddy!"

S C C

The two engines gazed at him side by side. He shut his eyes. "Are there *two* of you?" he whispered.

"Yes, we're twins."

"I might have known it," he groaned.

Just then, Edward bustled up. "Bill and Ben, why are you playing here?"

"We're *not* playing," protested Bill.

"We're rescuing trucks," squeaked Ben.

"What do you mean?"

"Even *you* don't come in our Yard without asking."

"And you only take the trucks we give you."

"But," they both squeaked indignantly, "this diseasel didn't even ask. He just took the lot!"

BRENDAM BAY
S C C
2

"There is no cause to be rude," said Edward severely. "This engine is a 'Metropolitan-Vickers, diesel-electric, Type 2.' "

The twins were abashed. "We're sorry Mr-er. . . . "

"Never mind," he smiled, "call me BoCo. I'm sorry I didn't understand about the trucks."

"That's all right then," said Edward. "Off you go, Bill and Ben. Fetch BoCo's trucks, then you can take these."

The twins scampered away. Edward smiled.

"There's no real harm in them," he said, "but they're maddening at times."

BoCo chuckled. "Maddening," he said, "is the word."

Buzz Buzz

BoCo reached the Big Station and arranged his trucks. Then he went to the Shed, and asked politely if he could come in.

Duck was not pleased to see a diesel but, presently, when he found that BoCo knew Edward, he became more friendly. And by the time BoCo had told him about Bill and Ben they were laughing together like old friends.

"Have they ever played tricks on *you*?" asked BoCo.

"Goodness me! Yes!" chuckled Duck. "Edward is the only one who can keep them in order."

"You know," went on Duck, "I sometimes call them 'The Bees'."

"A good name," chuckled BoCo. "They're terrors when they start buzzing round."

Just then James bustled in. "What's that, Duck? Are you terrified of bees? They're only insects after all: so don't let that buzz-box diesel tell you different."

"His name is BoCo, and he didn't. We . . . "

"I wouldn't care," interrupted James, "if hundreds were swarming round. I'd just blow smoke and make them buzz off."

"Buzz Buzz Buzz," retorted Duck.

James retired into a huff.

G W R

James was to pull the Express next morning, and when Duck brought his coaches the platform was crowded.

"Mind your backs! MIND YOUR BACKS!" Two porters were taking a loaded trolley to the front van. Fred drove, while Bert walked behind.

"Careful, Fred! Careful!" warned Bert, but Fred was in a hurry and didn't listen.

Suddenly an old lady appeared in front.

Fred stopped dead, but the luggage slid forward and burst the lid of a large white wooden box.

Some bees flew out, and, just as James came backing down, they began to explore the station.

Someone shouted a warning. The platform cleared like magic.

The bees were too sleepy to be cross. They found the empty station cold. James's Fireman was trying to couple the train. They buzzed round him hopefully. They wanted him to mend their hive. Then they could go back and be warm again.

But the Fireman didn't understand. He thought they would sting him.

He gave a yell, ran back to the cab and crouched with his jacket over his head.

The Driver didn't understand either. He swatted at the bees with the shovel.

The bees, disappointed, turned their attention to James.

James's boiler was nice and warm. The bees swarmed round it happily.

"Buzz off! BUZZ OFF!" he hissed. He made smoke, but the wind blew it away, and the bees stayed.

At last one settled on his hot smokebox. It burnt its feet. The bee thought James had stung it on purpose. It stung James back – right on the nose!

"Eeeeeeeeeeeeee!" whistled James. He had had enough: so had his Driver and Fireman. They started without waiting for the Guard's whistle.

They didn't notice till too late, that they'd left their train behind.

In the end it was BoCo who pulled the Express. He was worried at first about leaving his trucks, but Duck promised to look after them and so it was arranged. He managed to gain back some of the lost time, and the Fat Controller was pleased with him.

No one seemed to notice when James came back to the Shed. They were talking about a new kind of beehive on wheels. It was red, they said. Then they all said "Buzz, buzz, buzz," and laughed a lot.

James thought that for big Main Line Engines they were being very silly.

G W R

Wrong Road

THOMAS'S BRANCH LINE is important, and so is Edward's. They both bring in valuable traffic, but their track and bridges are not so strong as those on the Main.

That is why the Fat Controller does not allow the heavier Main Line Engines such as Gordon and Henry to run on them.

If, however, you had heard Gordon talking to Edward a short while ago, you would have thought that the Fat Controller had forbidden him to run on Branch Lines for quite another reason.

"It's not fair," grumbled Gordon.

"What isn't fair?" asked Edward.

"Letting Branch Line diesels pull Main Line trains."

"Never mind, Gordon. I'm sure BoCo will let you pull his trucks sometimes. That would make it quite fair."

Gordon spluttered furiously. "I *won't* pull BoCo's dirty trucks. I *won't* run on Branch Lines."

"Why not? It would be a nice change."

"The Fat Controller would never approve," said Gordon loftily. "Branch Lines are vulgar."

He puffed away in a dignified manner. Edward chuckled and followed him to the Station...

Gordon, his Driver and his Fireman all say it was the lady's fault. She wore a green floppy hat, and was saying "Goodbye" to a friend sitting in the coach nearest the Guard's Van.

It was almost time to start. The Fireman looked back. He was new to the job. He couldn't see the Guard but he did see something green waving. He thought it was the flag.

"Right away, Mate," he called.

But the Guard had not waved his flag. When Gordon started he left some luggage, several indignant passengers and the Guard all standing on the platform.

Every evening two fast trains leave the Big Station within five minutes. The 6.25 is Gordon's for the Main Line. Edward's, at 6.30, runs along the Branch.

By the time Gordon had been brought back, Edward's train was overdue.

"You've missed your 'path', Gordon", said the Fat Controller, crossly. "Now we must clear Edward's train before you can start."

This should have put everything right with the least possible trouble; but Control at the Big Station made things worse. They forgot to warn the signalman at Edward's Junction about the change of plan.

It was dark by the time the trains reached the Junction, and you can guess what happened – Edward went through on the Main, while Gordon was switched to the Branch . . . .

It took the Fat Controller several hours to sort out the tangle and pacify the passengers.

In the cnd Gordon was left, with his fire drawn, cold and cross on one of Edward's sidings.

Bill and Ben peeped into the Yard next morning. They wondered if BoCo had brought them some trucks. There were no trucks, but they didn't mind that.

Teasing Gordon, they thought, would be much better fun!

SODOR

"What's that?" asked Bill loudly.

"Ssh!" whispered Ben. "It's Gordon."

"It *looks* like Gordon, but it can't be. Gordon *never* comes on Branch Lines. He thinks them vulgar."

Gordon pretended he hadn't heard.

"If it isn't Gordon," said Ben, "it's just a pile of old iron . . . "

" . . . which we'd better take to the scrap-yard."

"No, Bill, this lot's useless for scrap. We'll take it to the harbour and dump it in the sea."

Gordon was alarmed. "I *am* Gordon. Stop! Stop!"

The twins paid no attention. Gordon shut his eyes and prepared for the worst.

BRENDAN BAY
SCC
BILL
SCC
BRENDAM BAY
2

The twins argued loudly and long. Bill favoured the scrapyard, while Ben said that the cutting up in such places was something cruel.

It would be kinder, he urged, to give these remains a quick end in the sea. Besides, he went on, they would make a lovely splash.

Gordon could not view either prospect with any enthusiasm.

Up to that time he had disapproved of diesels.

They were, he considered, ugly, smelly, and noisy; but when he opened his eyes and saw BoCo coming into the Yard, he thought him the most beautiful sight he had ever seen.

4
1

"BoCo my dear engine!" he gasped. "Save me!"

BoCo quickly sized up the situation, and sent Bill and Ben about their business.

They were cheeky at first, but BoCo threatened to take away the trucks of coal he had brought for them. That made them behave at once.

Gordon thought he was wonderful. "Those little demons!" he said. "How do you do it?"

"Ah well," said BoCo. "It's just a knack."

Gordon thinks to this day that BoCo saved his life; but we know that the twins were only teasing – don't we?

T L B
S C C

Edward's Exploit

EDWARD scolded the twins severely, but told Gordon it served him right. Gordon was furious.

A few days later, some Enthusiasts came. On their last afternoon they went to the China Clay Works.

Edward found it hard to start the heavy train.

"Did you see him straining?" asked Henry.

"Positively painful," remarked James.

"Just pathetic," grunted Gordon. "He should give up and be Preserved before it's too late."

"Shut up!" burst out Duck. "You're all jealous. Edward's better than any of you."

"You're right, Duck," said BoCo. "Edward's old, but he'll surprise us all."

Bill and Ben were delighted with their visitors. They loved being photographed and took the party to the Workings in a "Brakevan Special".

On the way home, however, the weather changed. Wind and rain buffeted Edward. His sanding gear failed, his wheels slipped, and his Fireman rode in front dropping sand on the rails by hand.

"ComeOn-ComeOn-ComeOn," panted Edward breathlessly. "This is dreadful!"

But there was worse to come. Before his Driver could check them, his wheels slipped fiercely again and again.

With a shrieking crack, something broke and battered his frame and splashers up and out of shape.

BRENDAM BAY
1
S C C
BILL

The passengers gathered round while the Crew inspected the damage. Repairs took some time.

"One of your crank-pins broke, Edward," said his Driver at last. "We've taken your side-rods off. Now you're a 'single' like an old fashioned engine. Can you get these people home? They must start back tonight."

"I'll try, Sir," promised Edward.

They backed down to where the line was more nearly level. Edward puffed and pulled his hardest, but his wheels kept slipping and he just could not start the heavy train.

The passengers were getting anxious.

2

Driver, Fireman and Guard went along the train making adjustments between the coaches.

"We've loosened the couplings, Edward," they said. "Now you can pick your coaches up one by one, just as you do with trucks."

"That will be much easier," said Edward gratefully.

So, with the Fireman sanding carefully in front, the Driver gently opened the regulator.

Come . . . on! puffed Edward. He moved cautiously forward, ready to take the strain as his tender coupling tightened against the weight of the first coach.

2

The first coach moving, helped to start the second, the second helped the third, and so on down the train.

"I've done it! I've done it!" puffed Edward, his wheels spinning with excitement.

"Steady, Boy!" warned his Driver, skilfully checking the wheel-slip. "Well done, Boy!"

"You've got them! You've *got* them!" And he listened happily to Edward's steady beat as he forged slowly but surely up the hill.

The passengers were thrilled. Most had their heads out of windows. They waved and shouted, cheering Edward on.

2

The Fat Controller paced the platform. Henry with the Special train waited anxiously too.

They heard a "Peep peep!" Then, battered, weary, but unbeaten, Edward steamed in.

The Fat Controller stepped angrily forward. He pointed to the clock, but excited passengers swept him aside. They cheered Edward, his Driver and Fireman to the echo, before rushing off to get in Henry's train.

Henry steamed away to another storm of cheers, but not before everyone knew Edward's story.

Edward went thankfully to the Shed, while Duck and BoCo saw to it that he was left in peace. Gordon and James remained respectfully silent.

2
2

The Fat Controller asked BoCo to look after Edward's line while he was being mended. BoCo was pleased. He worked well, and now they run it together. Bill and Ben still tease him, but BoCo doesn't mind.

He lives at Edward's Station, but is welcome anywhere, for he is now one of the "family".

Donald and Douglas were the last to accept him, but he often helps with their goods trains, and the other day they were heard to remark, "For a diesel, yon BoCo's nae sich a bad sort of engine."

That, from the Caledonian Twins, is high praise indeed!

COAL & COKE